Cami Kangaroo and Wyatt Too

Cami and Wyatt Share the Christmas Spirit

written by Stacy C. Bauer • illustrated by Rebecca Sinclair

Cami and Wyatt Share the Christmas Spirit
Cami Kangaroo and Wyatt Too
Published by Hop Off The Press, LLC
www.stacycbauer.com
Minneapolis, MN

Library of Congress Control Number: 2020915439
Bauer, Stacy C. Author
Sinclair, Rebecca Illustrator
Cami and Wyatt Share the Christmas Spirit

ISBN: 978-0-9998141-6-1

JUVENILE FICTION

All inquiries of this book can be sent to the author.
For more information or to book an event, please visit www.stacycbauer.com

For my Savior Jesus, the true meaning of Christmas,
my mom, the most selfless person I know
and my kids, Cami and Wyatt,
the best Christmas gifts I've ever received.
-S.C.B.

For my friends and family, who are a constant
reminder of what the holidays are really all about.
-R.S.

With only 17 days until Christmas, the Kangaroo house was busy.

Mommy and Daddy were hanging Christmas lights outside while Cami and Wyatt were hunched over the toy catalog making their Christmas lists.

"Ooh, look at this easel, Wyatt! I've always wanted one of these to paint on," Cami exclaimed.

"Wow! I want this soccer ball!" They spent the rest of the day looking through the toys.

On the school bus the next morning, all of their friends were talking about what they wanted for Christmas. Cami told her friends about the easel.

"I'm asking Santa for a new video game!" Malcolm exclaimed.
"I want some books!" Audrey said.
"Me too!" said Olivia. "And some stuffed animals."
"I want a new soccer ball!" Wyatt added.

As they chattered excitedly, Cami noticed that not everyone was joining in. A few seats up, she recognized her new neighbors Violet and Chester Koala.

"Hi, I'm your neighbor Cami. What do you want for Christmas?" Cami asked.
Violet shrugged shyly.

"Let's ask Violet to sit with us at lunch," Cami suggested. Olivia and Audrey agreed. "We should ask Chester to play with us at recess," Malcolm said. Wyatt nodded.

Cami saw Violet sitting alone eating a bag lunch, but when she started toward her, Violet picked up her lunch and left.

During recess, Cami and her friends noticed Violet sitting on the swings by herself. Recess ended just as Cami and her friends were about to ask Violet to play.

Wyatt and Malcolm went to ask Chester to build a snow fort, but he ran off.

That afternoon, Cami and Wyatt sat by the koalas on the bus.

"Hi," they said.
"Hi," Chester said quietly.
"When did you move in?" Wyatt asked.
"Last week," Chester answered.

Cami and Wyatt wanted to talk more, but the bus arrived at their stop.

"Mommy," Wyatt asked at dinner that night,
"do you know the new neighbors?"
"You mean the Koala family?" Mommy asked.
"Yeah," Wyatt said, then sighed.
"What's wrong?" Daddy asked.

"They looked lonely, so we sat by them on the bus, but they didn't really talk to us," Wyatt said, frustrated. "We tried to play with Chester at recess, but he ignored us!"

"Well," Mommy said, "maybe they're shy. After all, they just moved in."

"Don't give up on them," Daddy agreed. "Mommy and I will go over there and introduce ourselves to their parents soon."

Christmas was approaching quickly. The Kangaroo family put up their Christmas tree and hung the stockings.

They went shopping for gifts for family and friends, and got their pictures taken with Santa.

Cami's List
• Easel
• magic markers
• Books
• camera
• CANDY

Wyatt's List
• Soccerball
• video games
• comic Books
• etch Book
• il Set

Cami and Wyatt added to their Christmas lists.

Cami and Wyatt tried talking to the Koalas a couple more times at school, but they gave short answers and kept turning away.

That weekend, Cami and Wyatt made Christmas cookies with Mommy.

Later, they watched as their parents brought the Koala family the cookies.

When Mommy and Daddy came back, they sat down with Cami and Wyatt in the living room.

"Their parents are very nice," Daddy said.
"They moved here because their daddy had to find a different job. It seems like things are hard for them right now," Mommy explained.

Cami thought about Violet's holey backpack and bag lunch and Chester's taped glasses.

"We've been going on and on about all of the stuff we want for Christmas," Cami groaned.
"That's probably why they won't talk to us," Wyatt said, sadly.

"Maybe they felt left out or embarrassed because they don't have much money right now," Cami stated.

"But Christmas isn't about how much money you have or how many gifts you get!" Wyatt exclaimed.

"It's about family and friends and being kind!" Cami chimed in.
"It sounds like you're starting to figure out the true meaning of Christmas," Mommy observed.
"Don't give up on those little Koalas. They'll come around."

Over the next week, Cami and Wyatt spent time getting to know Violet and Chester.

They sat by them on the bus,

invited them to eat lunch with them

and played with them at recess.

The Kangaroo family took the Koala family
window shopping down Main Street,

decorated gingerbread houses with them

and invited them along
to the town's tree lighting
ceremony.

It was the last day of school before Christmas break and the bus was buzzing with excitement.

"Remember when we made that gingerbread house and ate half of the candy?" Cami asked Violet.

That was so fun!" she agreed. "I liked walking downtown, too. The smells coming out of that bakery...mmm."

"My family and I had fun singing Christmas carols around the town tree," Audrey said.
Olivia chimed in, "The lights were so colorful and pretty."

As they got off the bus, Violet quietly said, "I'm sorry we weren't very friendly at first. We were nervous about being friends with you all because we don't have much money right now."

"You don't need money to have friends...or fun!"
Cami quickly made a snowball and launched it at the boys.
They both burst out laughing.

The Kangaroos and the Koalas spent the next few days together spreading Christmas cheer in their neighborhood.

They shoveled driveways,

hung wreaths on doors

and delivered cookies to the mail carriers.

They collected toys for kids
who didn't have any,

helped serve a holiday
dinner at church

and went caroling door to door.

Cami and Wyatt woke up Christmas morning to the smell of cinnamon rolls baking.

They hopped down the stairs to see filled stockings and gifts under the tree.
The Kangaroo family was just about to open their gifts, when the doorbell rang.

They opened the door to find
the Koala family with
homemade cards and gifts.

"Merry Christmas!"
the Koalas chimed.

They invited the
Kangaroos to begin
a new tradition with
them—an annual
snow fort and
snowman building
competition.

While building a fort with their new friends, Cami and Wyatt thought about the true meaning of Christmas:

family, friends and spreading joy to others.

"This is the best Christmas yet!"
Cami said, gleefully.

Everyone agreed.

About the Author

Stacy C. Bauer is the award-winning author of the *Cami Kangaroo and Wyatt Too* children's book series. She is also a teacher and mom, has been writing since she was a child and loves sharing stories of her kids' antics and making people laugh. Stacy lives in a suburb of Minneapolis with her husband and two children, Cami and Wyatt, the inspiration behind her writing.

You can find out more about Stacy and her books at www.stacycbauer.com

About the Illustrator

Rebecca Sinclair is the illustrator of the *Cami Kangaroo and Wyatt Too* children's book series. She received her MFA in children's book illustration from the Academy of Art University in San Francisco.

You can find Rebecca creating kangaroos and other furry characters in Grand Rapids, Michigan with her french bulldog, Phoebe.
To view more of Rebecca's work, visit her website at www.rebeccasinclairstudio.com

Christmas Acts of Kindness

1. Donate food to your food pantry. Take some time to explain why families might need to use a food bank and then go shopping together. Let the children pick out most of the items. If possible have them accompany you when you drop the food off at the food bank.
2. Take supplies to an animal shelter.
3. Save up some change and put it in the Salvation Army bucket.
4. As a family, choose a charity to give to or a family to bless with little surprises throughout the holiday season.
5. Take part in a local charitable service such as Santa's Anonymous or Toys For Tots.
6. Deliver or donate blankets to those who sleep in the cold.
7. Assemble blessing bags for the homeless.
8. Leave a gift and card for your mail carrier.
9. Have a family baking party and make your favorite treats. Then give them to people that work for the community, such as nurses, teachers, police, and fire-fighters.
10. Write thank you notes to people who go all out to decorate their yard and house with lights. Thank them for lighting up the neighborhood.
11. Do yard work or shovel snow for a neighbor.
12. Take a Christmas plant to someone who doesn't get outside very much.

3. Sing Christmas carols/songs for your neighbors.
4. Make or buy a bird feeder.
5. Make Christmas cards out of recycled art work and use them to write some notes to nursing home residents or children in the hospital.
6. Candy cane bomb a parking lot. It's simple! Just go around sticking candy canes and a note on car windshields for people to discover. Coffee Cups and Crayons has a free printable to help. Want something even simpler? Candy cane bomb your immediate neighbors!
7. Make some kindness rocks to leave around the neighborhood or a local park.

Made in United States
North Haven, CT
15 November 2022

26789268R00022